T0148552

Inspirations
AND *Things*
TO THINK ABOUT

Inspirations
AND *Things*
TO THINK ABOUT

RICKY EL

INSPIRATIONS AND THINGS TO THINK ABOUT

iUniverse books may be ordered through booksellers or by contacting:

iUniverse
1663 Liberty Drive
Bloomington, IN 47403
www.iuniverse.com
1-800-Authors (1-800-288-4677)

ISBN: 978-1-5320-7464-6 (sc)
ISBN: 978-1-5320-7465-3 (e)

Print information available on the last page.

iUniverse rev. date: 07/11/2019

Blow Away Darkness

Darkness is
"Fear" - in forms
We wait for light
The coming dawn
To winds "blow away"
Our imagining minds
And in this light, "Our"
"Peace" we find.

Upon my mind,
These things
I think,
Imagination images
Inside, I drink,
To walk upon
Another's thoughts
Sometime, inside
We all get lost

On moon light, tides
On blue oceans foams
White sandy, beaches, I walk
All alone

What's, in the wind
Hopes, and dreams,
Fears, of dying,
Imaginiveity thing,
I can see, love
Some day,
But for right now,
No way

Falling snow
A bright summers day
In my heart
Their singing
I like it that way

A budding flower
Stands, still, in the
Suns light
While growing
In the dark night

Would you like
To walk with me
Back in time
To enitys
We can no longer find

I am a butterfly
Flittering my wings
Flying on high - and
Landing on things

My favorite things
Too land on, are, flowering
Buds, at the beak of sunlight

I land then I suck the juices
Then, I take flight
Once, again into the air
There I go
To find me - a female butterfly
I might want to know

Ocean waves
With white billowing caps
Move rhythmically
Onto, white sands
Bringing, life, from, fathoms, depths
Upon the blue covering
Of earths, dark, and brownish, land.

Hello world
I say
Trying to maintain
Another day
I see no place
But jet I try
To keep and
Maintain and render
A balanced mind

What's your dreams
Do you have hope
Goals to fulfill
Plans and scopes
We try to have a
Better life
An onward go
Through toil and strife

What can we say
To humanity's needs
To help and assist
We cloth and we feed
To lift our hearts high
And do what we can
All to preserve - the civilization of man

I awoke
This morning
From my sleep
Took a deep
Breath,
Opened my eyes - to peep
And saw myself, I got the creeps

Beautiful day isn't it
I said
As I pass another's head
Hope it don't, rain,
We need some sunshine
To lighten up the
Our hearts and minds

With all that's happening
In the world today
It's very hard to keep, straight
Your way
To navigate
Life's, strange passageway
And to succeed at goals
Each and everyday

Legends
Legends of heroes
Strong and brave
Valiantly
Saving those,
Weak and afraid
A way of life
We used to know
Now blowing, away
In the winds, that
Blow.

Where in darkness
Do we find
The light.
In the heart
In the mind
In our souls
At night
A question
I ponder
With all of
My might

Beautiful
A mountain top
With white caps peaks
A pitch black night,
With starry, bright lights
Surrounded by
Evergreen trees, an
Within their circle,
A moons lit light.

An occupied, white
Tropical, sandy beach
With emerald green an
See through blue, ocean
Surrounded sea.
Billowing white clouds
Over head, a margarita
In thy hand, while I
Rest my head. For sleep
With you

I lost a love
Today
My heat is broken
But luckily
I seen the feeling
Before
I formore day
Unspoken

Why do I get watched
All the time
Or is this just
My imagining mind
I seem to walk
In day jah vour'
While others pass me
And try to look into
How they think
I am
And sum up an estimation
Of their imaginationing mind
Of what I am

What's with
These ideas now
That don't match
What I think "somehow"
Is this a sign,
Of changing time
It seems to - rack my soul
Or is this, just nature
Saying, your just getting old

I woke up this
Morning
To the sounds of a bird
That sang
And it seemed that in
It heart, it was happy
The way the melody rang
Cheerful up beat, a melodious
Tune
That brightened my day
And chased away
My gloom.

Where to get too
What should, I do
Step into
Fantasy,
Maybe make my
Dreams come true
I think I will
I think I won't
Who, know
As I sail
Upon my sailing boat

I planted some, flowers
The other day
Immediately they
Grew, an towards
The sun they played
And the life they
Inspired
Was all very good
To water and nourish
Something
And then their life
Stood

A cat came to me
Straight to my hand
And bowed its head
And I rubbed its
Head, neck, and face
We find much beauty
In such a small place.

Hi said thee, lady
I passed today
And then she said
I hope you have a good
Day, simplicity in so
Many ways.

Have you ever
Got caught up
In a turbine of thoughts
Look inside them
And get lost
Well I do, even if you don't
Some say - you will and
Others say you won't

What's with thee weather
I mean the weatherman
He tell me "this"
"And I," make my plans
He says "rainy today"
That the news
So I get my umbrella
And rain day shoes
I prepare to get out
And behold in my face
The sun is so bright
I can't see a darn thing

Mountains and flower
Winds and rain
Clouds and sunshine
With beautiful - things
Black starry night
With the moon 'shining'
Down," so wonderfully bright
Between the clouds

Poetry

Sweet is the sound
Of dice
"As they, turn over
Your number
Twice

Coming brushing
Cleaning, is what
Feel nice
And thinking about
Thee ladies
That your going to get
Tonight.

I said what up
What up
To my catatonic
Friend
Half way, falling in, his
Drunken, stumbling
Binge, I said can you
See my man,
Before you fall - again
Do you need, some help
And then he passed out
Again

One thing
I like
Is
City suits
For no matter
What the time
Of day
A suit - is a suit
It uplifts
My mind, and helps
Me think of higher thing
Like helping humanity
From tyranny and
Pain.

How's your wife
How's your mother
How's your sister, and brothers
Friend
I hope your family's
Doing good
And not like Robin Hood

Animals at the (city zoo)
There just so many thing
I notice - can't you see
One are, the animal
That surround me,
The monkey, causing mischief
All day long, the lions
Quiet, but don't, take them
Wrong
The snakes are, more
Slippery, subtle can't you
See, kinds of reminds me
Of people that around me.

What's good, what band
What's up what's down
My man, - and do they
Still have bad elements
The this part of town

You'd better, pay attention
To this thing called time
It grinds away slowly,
Your life and it's on yours
And mine
Never stopping, never dropping
Bite by bite

When will I get
A break
It's been quite awhile
Now, I think the last
One, was when I was
A child.

The smell of colon, or perfume
When it's just right
Can take you to wonders
And beautiful delights
Of hopeful things, of imaginations dreams
To sultry, provocative, and some times
Sexual things.
And then it's gone,
With memories of the past, and
Only a faint fragrance left
That fades fast.

Here's our hopes here's are dreams
Trying to obtain then
Is a mysterious thing, we try we try
Until it comes to pass
And with our hearts, in our hands
We hope it will last

All in all
What's the difference
We all seem, to say
A half a pound of one
Or the other, it can go
Either way.

Off to work another day
Still a little tired from
Yesterday, some routine
Some grind, no time for
Others - only the work time
Can't what till it end, and
Then it starts all over again

Winter, snow, and cold
The things that freezes things
Makes them move faster
To a more heated environmental
Plane

A puppy dogs life
Twisty, panty, running
Barking life. I guess that's
Alright.

Butterflies
I like to see
Butterflies
Their soft, fast flippings
Through the air
Stopping, to, rest, or, stopping
On a flower, somewhere
To taste the nectar inside there.

By the time
We plant a flower
Place it in the soil
Add fertilizer, earth
Water, and its feeds
From that moment it
Toils, to reach down its
Roots, to strive to
Life a natural, complimentary
Life.

There's lighting, and
Thunder, wind and rain
And still I wonder
Who's there, they say

"Love"
What's, this love
Anyway
Some kind of feeling
They all say.
It seems to be
And never, ending
Sear

So this the
Ways of life
Man if I knew that
I'd of stay where I
Was at
Because living here can
Be beautiful,
And also hit you flat

"Where's the love
When people
Want their money
"Where's the love
When people are
Tired and frustrated
Where the love.
I think it's something, their not thinking of

What happen
To the child
Who's born
Into a war torn
Family,
Mother broken,
Daddy's bad
What happen to him
Or will he last - good or bad?

What up with (money)
They seem to all want more
Rested out, stressed out
Only got money on the brain
Some take, some break, others
Are torn, other lay on the
Side way, humiliated and scorned

If I had a nickel
For my every thoughts
I'd wish the world
Peace and happiness
And never, be hungry
Or lost.

What I can't see
Is posers, exploiter
Pretender, offender
Minds demented, and
The I need a quarter
Sir-ers the greedy
Conceded, the my
Agenda I am feeding
Get out of my way.
And thee I don't care
If your bleeding, please - get away from me.

If I were, just
A butterfly, a caterpillar,
Or a fly,
I am just a part of
Nature, trying to exist.

What's so simple
It will last, disappear
But will return, fast,
It's all around you
Never going away its
Just simplistic, we call
It rainy days

Meditation, is good
For the soul, it recharges
All the cell, and molecules
Of our physical mold.

Heavenly is a state
Of mind
Never let other break
Your piece of mind
Stay in heaven and don't
Fall down
And your paradise will
Away be around

Hearts are broken
Many cry, they deeply hurt
But heal
In time

Pieces of time
Whispers of minds
Memories of perfumes
A hug that one
Finds, all gone
Our maybe not

High roller
Here we are
Rolling the dice
A superstar
7 Eleven
Is what your
And money galore
Is what will be

Hello God
It's another day
I thank thee Lord
For a place to play

Some say living is hard
Other say living is good
I am just an observer
To me complications
Is good

I hope that all you
See an do
Gets better everyday
For happiness is hard
To find exactly as it
Should

It's all about
What you do
To do the good
And make it
Through

The world
Need compassion
The world needs
Cares,
To survive, all that's
Happening
We all must share

To help one another
Is the means of life
To do good for each other
Brings fulfilment to ones
Life

All and all
Oceans tide, brings
In food, and life
Before our eyes

I would like
To go to Jamaica,
Aruba, Cuba, the Caribbean
My imagination wonder
What there in that
Strange land

Have you ever really
Wanted to do somethings
You wish you could do
Like swing in the beaches
Of the Costa Rica shore

If only I had a genies
Lamp,
I wish good for that I can
And enjoy a fairly good life
Away in places
With stars at night

My dreams I need to make
For once, to come true
After all, it took to
Imagine them, and now
They try to bake

Incomplete, things
Are like, left overs
On a plate, we put
Them in a refrigerator
But the, cold and ice
Sucks away their, "taste"

With all I've, done
Nothing has, been
Done, so more I must
Do for "isn't" life
About this helping
Each other
For what we do
Or strive for - in our
Heart come true

What is "a moment"
Is it something
That is fast
Or is it suspended time
Or maybe (just stopped)
"In stillness"
Is this a moment - of
Bliss.

Even the animal
Knows, who an
When to call
They know, the gestures
Of how and when, to
Fall, to bow for honor
Or subjection of their
Presence of others big
Or small.

A (½ a pound
Of this, an a quarter
Pound of that, when
It all added up
It's called an even match

Here to the living
An my respects to the
Dead, for all pasts
Forgivings, until, stones
Graves are our beds
But think not of deeds, done
And in yesterdays, fade"
While your skeleton, skull
Lies rotting "in your grave

Love life
And live it, to the
Utmost, for only
"One" do you have"
Its time is short
An in one second
Of time it's gone.

Fun to me
Is have a pool stick
Between my hands
Shooting in an 8 ball
On the next man.

What do you "like"
I like fishing.
Maybe you don't
I like getting things done
Maybe you don't
I like, a beautiful
Sunset, on a blue, white
Sea.
Maybe you don't like
These things
Our maybe it's just me

(Fantasies)
Sometimes I fantasize
About a beautiful place
That's mine
Or a dog or cat, or a horse
I have
With plenty of room to run
Around
With a beautiful view during day
And a beautiful black starry night
Yes these yes these
Things I like

"Help me" help me
Is what comes to my mind
I don't have any "sugar"
For this oatmeal of mine
I already "cook it"
Now what "am I to do"
Cause oatmeal get hard
Just like glue.

The more I do
The more, that get done
The less I need
For under the sun

Where is the
Happiness
I don't see it around
It like it fading
And all the people
Have grimaces, or frowns

If heaven
Had a door
And within "it doors" lies
All of the
Angels,
That by God, "they "did" obid"
And with ideal
It's true
The earth be a better place
Then I think
It's all good,
Let's give them space.

"Children"
Are a blessing
And by God
I know that's true
For their
Innocent, and love
They give to me and you
And only wish to
To hold your hand
An for you,
To hold them "in your arms"
And, "for all the love they give
I love their innocent charms.

"Hot"
(Pancakes,) or waffles," instead
"Smother" in syrup
With butter on their head
Melting delicious
With fried chicken on
The side,
No don't look at me, with those, big brown eyes
Yours not getting, any.
Mine mine mine - all mine-

Jeepers
I need
Sneaker,
I need a pair, of shoes
The one I got
Are busted out
Now so what I am I to do

"What" - I am thinking
About that
"Light," kiss
I got last
Night
From that "girl"
I really kind of like"

Stop, stop, stop,
Right there
I saw you
Looking in that window
At my new pair of shoes
Don't think your going to get them
I am telling you
Cause tomorrow,
I am going to buy - those shoes

Here's
To a gambler
And a hustlers life
I wish all success
And all goes well
And all your games
Pay well in life

If time is an essence
Then what do we have
It's the only thing
Left after we pass
It get all, we've had
And have an then, it's
The only thing that
Wins.

Where are we at
I said to myself
In my head,
I must be lost
I turn an toss
I am I a sleep
I am I awake
For God's sake
Oh there I am

"Sincerity"
Something that's
Hard to find
In these days
With egotistic mind
Narcissistic, people and
Glamour - is all you
See, with pretentious
Bodies - is all you
Meet.

Flowers grow
They soak in the rain
Stretch out to the
Sunshine, an from the
Sunlight they drain
The sunbeams,
To grow up high
And produce their
Pollen - to float through
The sky.

In the
Sands of the beach
We find, sea shells
Muscles, clams, and whatever dwells
And white foam of
The oceans tide
And with these things
We abide.

Oh
Where, can I find
A patromy on rye
With extra onions
With sweet pickles on the side
With lots of other extras
That I dare not name
Nutritious for the belly
And delicious for the brain

What would life be, if we
Couldn't do what we like.
Like, bowling, shooting pool, or
Fishing at night,
Or taking a look of a fine lady
As she walks by
My oh my oh my oh my.

Summers coming
And then, in the
Son's light, the
Love bug will come out
At night, he stay in the
Pillows, and in the bed
He lays, waiting for night
To come out an play.

Are you ready - for summer
And all of is delights, to meet
Someone special, to share a
Bottle of wine, and a conversation
That's nice, (summer fairies) work
Their magic, "when" least you suspect
And maybe in an unsuspected moment
You'll be their elect- to fall under-
Their spell and then who knows
A light into your life - may be
Your rose.

It's good, so what can you say
All good, on this beautiful
Cloudy day

Man
It's hot, as, bezalbubs hells
I am sweating, bullet,
Big as thumb nails
Losing my breath,
Can't think - right
I feel, like I am going to
Fall out
From the light

A smooth cold, deep
In the swimming pool
Came to mind
Or relaxing in a sauna
With a glass of wine

Man I hate, "the cold"
"Freezing rain" frost, and snow
I don't care, what you
Say, I need to be in
Sunny, Florida today.
Watching all "the honey's
Strutting their curves
As they walk away

Work, work work
That all I do
Twenty four seven
Seven days a week
All I do is stop to
Eat, and maybe get
Some sleep.

Loyalty, honor, devotion, and pride
Has all been replaced
With mine, mine, mine,
Greed, and thievery
Has all come to pass
Glamour, pretentiousness,
Narcissism, has taken over
The past.
So here we are, a new era of man
And I really think he, doesn't give
A (ham)

Something right about the world
My daughters eye, when she reaches out and
Says dad, and hold me tight, and
Together we laugh.

"Perception"
All's not the same
Some say let run, to the light
Oth say, I can't see! It where
Can that be,
Down 6 blocks on 45 Street.

You've got to good "It's a chose that you have
Or your gonna be bad
Not from choosing
But from the people you might meet
That's just crazy and mad.

I see people "drinking every day"
As if "This will chase your their problems
Away.
My heart goes out for the those (in conflict)
But they only make themselves, put amongst
The rejects, - and rejected)

Hi Sir
How life treating you this day I said
And he replied, all is well - with God on my
Side.

Under the sea
Beneath the deep
Other creatures lurk
And lye in the dirt
Things were not seen
Or even know, creature
Who live in their own abodes

Clouds
You know that clouds
Make faces, forms
Things we can see
If we look for them

Wet weather
"Man" its raining out
Pouring down rain
Soaking up and into
Everything
It need to stop - cause I need
Some sun
Man I am done

Is it true
Another, (Icon) gone wrong
An then another
(Politician), another (Priest)
Another (Leader) another (Police)
Committing some heinous crime
For all to see
In a world of cracked mentalities
All who have succumbed to an
Darkness, and depravities

Where to find "happiness"
Some find happiness, in a kitten
Or a cat, others in horses
Or a polo match
Some find happiness in a woman's
Eyes, others, in a child's mind.

I can't stopping thinking about
That special shoot, in pool in dip
When I was hot
An about this lady - who gave me the
Eye, and throw in for extra
That smile

What I like most
Is a ginseng with honey "drink"
A pacific salmon, on toast
Within a casino that I like
The most.

Yes
I like to own
A Henley - sail boat yacht schooner
And a beach home mansion
My own hotels, an motels - (businesses) just
For expansion.

Do you dream - an if you do
Do you believe dreams come true
I am just asking, inquiring minds
Needs to know
Cause maybe your living one
Of your dreams - come true - sooo
Who knew.

I like to see fish, yes indeed in Florida
295 varieties, an type you see, so many kinds
To say the least,
And by far the best is catch and release

Have you ever
Been inebriated,
I mean way down in the slumps
And wake up
The next morning
Like you've woken up in the
Dumps

I've noticed that this
Desire - of (not hearing)
Runs rapidly amongst those -
With the (I don't care attitude) and the
(I don't have time to listen to you)
Have you too noticed that.
So I've asked God to forgive them for that,

Young girls play with doll babies, an
Young boy play with gun
And when they both hear
The sounds of the, ice cream truck
They both start, to run
I wish the world,
Happiness every day
And all the world problems solved right away.

You never know
What the day
Might bring
Your cup in the morning
And gone.
But the encounters that
You have, "last on and on."

Snow is beautiful and white
Blanket the ground
And makes it cold
During the night,
It covers you cars
Your houses, the trees
And most of all buries you
Up to your knees

All is well, as the clock
Strikes twelve, and all of magic
Steps in
For twelve is the bewitching hour
And strange things
Start to happen
No lie-s

Carousels
And carousel rides
Something from the past
That go up and down
With lights that shine
All around

Why do we "ponder"
I mean think and wonder
Get caught up in,
Which way to go
Is this decision right
Should we try it, maybe
I don't know, - tomorrow night

Fantasies
Believe - ability, or what
Can we really explain if
It's real, or not
So where do we stand on
In this particular spot

Wow! Wow! Wow!
Which way do I turn
And which way do I go

All we have
Are our dreams
Cause without those
What would we be
To contemplate - who, or
What we might be, have, or achieve
Or even see.

What's your color today
Blue, white, brown maybe red
Yes just a splash of red on your head
Maybe with grey.
Or some brown to match
You down
Oh yes what is the color today
Inside of my mind - it's what
He says.

How about - a night out
No - but it's been so long
How about a night out
You know it been to long
It's time to dance socialize and
Prance, if only until - dawn

I become happy
With the children
I see in the day
There full of hopes
And they want, what
They see -
But mostly they like
To play.

Is candor, a manner
In which we should
Live sharp to the point
Word that cut, through
Your emotions, and make
You see through the mirages
In which some exist.

Where oh where did I put
That, it go so perfect with
My Stetson cap, I can't
Seem to find, them, hum
Let me think
Oh there they are
My Ruby cuff links

Assumptions)
"I am" very, very, very
Cautious about (assumptions)
They are and do (chaos)
Is the things that they bring and
Intervene, to me and you
And cause problems, "it's very very
"mean," hurtful - and disturbs too

It's summer
All over again
And warm is here
Warming up women an men
It feel good
And about time
For the bite of Jack Frost
Got into my soul

Well well well
What do we have here
A little girl is crying and
Dropping all these tears
I said don't cry, little one
And thanks for all your tear
They make the flowers bloom
And brings summer nearer

Here I seat
Between dimensions
In this open places I dwell - cause
They won't take me
In heaven
An won't except me in hell
Now this is my conundrum
As I set here alone or
Until God decides,
Which one will be my home

Yes
I like the smell of honey suckles
In June, and the stories we were
Told, of the cow, jumping over the moon
And of Humpty Dumpty - who had a
Great fall who fell from off of that great wide
Wall, - but mostly I like, the stars that
Shine at night

"Mirror" Mirror hanging there, don't you see me
Don't you care. I can see you,
But you can't see me, what there's a person
No that can't be, there right there, between the glass
Oh it's only me.

When one opens up their minds
Their usually on their way to
Find what they need
In their lives and time, immediately

I've learned to, look at the
Moment, and "enjoy"
To take in all - the things
And get comfortable with
How things might be as we live

Some times we get a sensuous day
A day when all the ladies
Look your way
They all seem to be there
A get you
That special stare

Last night I dreamed
That I could dance, and in a
Ball room floor
I pranced, swirling, whirling
To the dance, and
You'll never know how long my
Smile did last

Printed in the United States
By Bookmasters